This book belongs to:

Elliott James
with love, Amber

Bedtime Stories

8 timeless tales
by Margaret Wise Brown

Bath • New York • Cologne • Melbourne • Delhi
Hong Kong • Shenzhen • Singapore

This edition published by Parragon Books Ltd in 2017
and distributed by

Parragon Inc.
440 Park Avenue South, 13th Floor
New York, NY 10016
www.parragon.com

Written by Margaret Wise Brown
Additional cover illustrations by Carrie May
Edited by Emma Horridge
Designed by Anna Madin
Production by Danielle Nevin

ISBN 978-1-4723-9193-3

Printed in China

Contents

The Noon Balloon

Illustrated by
Lorena Alvarez

A girl and boy wished they could fly,
On a magical journey through the sky.

They climbed aboard the Noon Balloon!
It was swift as the wind and round as the moon.

Where would they travel, and what would they do,
Floating through the skies so blue?

7

Over the treetops and far away,
Over the sea where the mermaids play.

They whooshed along on a galloping breeze,
Sailing above waves and swirling seas.

A land of clover stretched pink and sweet,
They heard bees buzz and songbirds tweet.

A dragonfly flashed up, ready to play,
Then sped ahead to show them the way.

Onward they flew through the bright, clear air,
Over valleys and hills, though they knew not where.

"Look!" said the boy, who had spotted a clown.
Then they heard distant cheers from a circus in town.

Six little balloons floated up from below
They danced in the air as if saying hello.

"Blow away!" called the clown, and what else could they do?
They caught the breeze and away they flew.

14

Where were they going? Would they get there soon?
On through the sky flew the Noon Balloon . . . .

15

Then suddenly, the clouds grew dark,
And the little dog began to bark.

Great gold lightning split the sky!
Whirling, swirling, way up high.

The little girl shouted, "Hold on tight!"
They grabbed the ropes with all their might.

The Noon Balloon was rocked and spun!
Then, just like that, out popped the sun.

Biff! And bang! Smoke filled the sky.
Below them cars went whizzing by.

Shiny buildings left and right.
The air was thick; the lights were bright.

The city's rhythm, like a drum,
Chug-a-rum, chug-a-rum, chug-a-rum, chug-a-rum.

They left the city far behind
For more exciting things to find!

Now way up high, a brrr and roar!
They saw an airplane dip and soar.

Backward, forward, here and there,
Airplanes, airplanes everywhere!

And then there were no sounds at all,
As the golden sun began to fall.

Past magical gardens of roses and mint,
Where water sparkles and fireflies glint.

The afternoon was deep and warm.
A thin white moon began to form.

The Noon Balloon then stopped and bowed,
Descending softly as a cloud.

They'd reached an unfamiliar land,
An ancient forest, tall and grand.

A secret village; what a sight!
One hundred candles burning bright.

Tiny houses in the trees,
Nestled snug between the leaves.

They played all night, then played some more,
So high above the forest floor.

And when the dawn began to show,
A restless wind began to blow.

They climbed once more into the skies,
While a golden sun began to rise.

26

They knew where to go, and they'd get there soon.
Back through the sky flew the Noon Balloon.

the Find it Book

Illustrated by
Lisa Sheehan

Find the **honey** and **plenty** of money.

Find the Owl and the Pussycat.

Find the **hole** where a stitch in time saves nine.

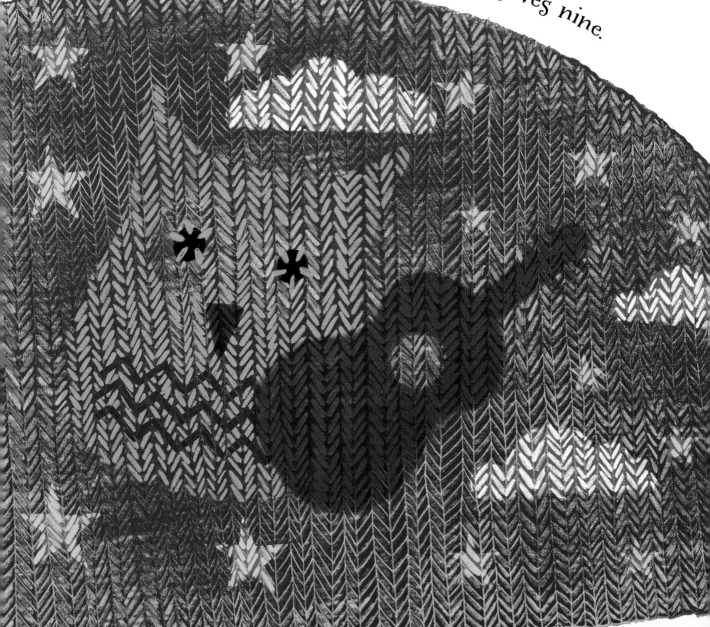

33

Find Little Bo Peep's lost sheep.

Find the **wolf** in sheep's clothing.

Find the **little piggy** that went to the market.

Find the **little piggy** that went
wee-wee-wee all the way home.

3 miles

Find the **crooked man** who walked a crooked mile.

39

Find the **COW** that jumped over the moon.

40

Find the **dish** that ran away with the **spoon**.

Find Humpty Dumpty sitting on the wall

42

Find the **mouse** that ran up the clock.

43

Find the Itsy Bitsy Spider

climbing up the waterspout.

Find Georgie Porgie, pudding and pie.

Find the **child** who had her cake and ate it, too.

Find the twinkle, twinkle, little star.

Find the **man in the moon.**

Find your **favorite!**

The DIGGERS

Illustrated by

Antoine Corbineau

DIG
DIG

A mole was digging a hole.

DIG DIG DIG

A dog was digging a hole
under a stone to bury a bone.

DIG DIG

DIG

A worm was digging a hole.

He swallowed the ground,

as he wiggled around,

56

and ate his way toward home.

DIG
DIG
DIG

A rabbit was digging a hole,

next to a mouse,
who was digging a house,

in a little warm hole
in the ground.

59

DIG
DIG
DIG

In the city, a man was digging a hole.

Monday he dug,

Tuesday he dug,

61

And then came the big digger,
    made by a man to dig deeper and bigger,

To scoop up stones,
and find dinosaur bones,
and cavemen's homes,
and buried gnomes.

63

DIG
DIG
DIG

The shovel dug its way.
Night after night,
day after day

it dug.

And a great big hole ran under the city,
under a river,
and into the bright green country.

A man put a train in the hole.

And the train ran under the street, under the city, under the river, until

66

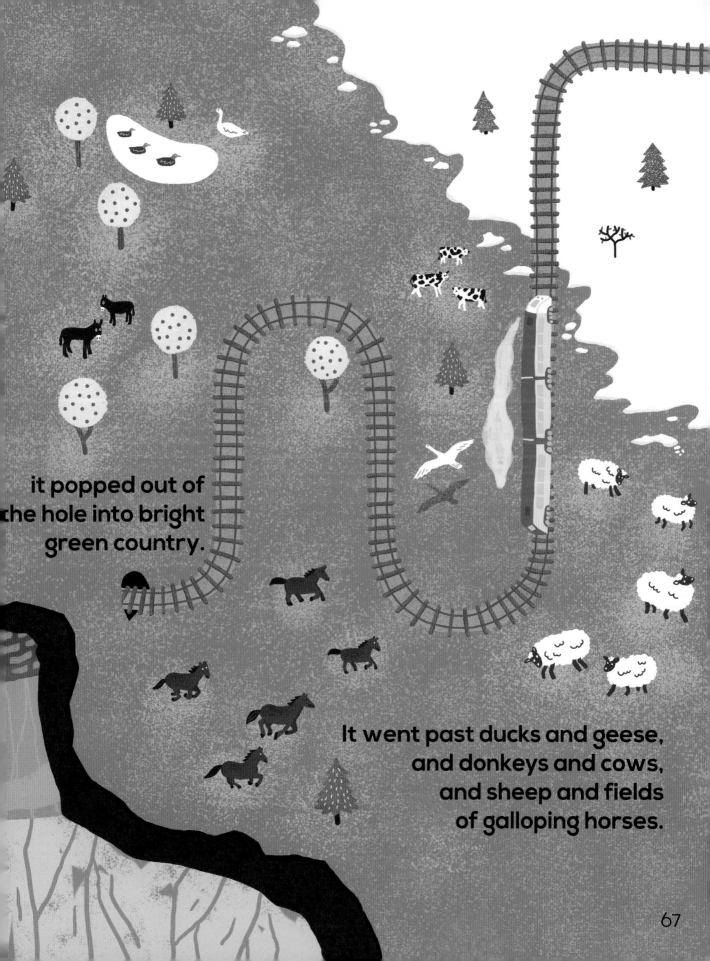

it popped out of
the hole into bright
green country.

It went past ducks and geese,
and donkeys and cows,
and sheep and fields
of galloping horses.

67

Until it came to a mountain

and couldn't get over

and couldn't get through

and couldn't get around.

And so it had to stop.
But not forever.

69

For down the track came another train.
And on the last car rode the great digger.

Under the mountain, it dug away,
night after night, day after day.

Until, with one last bite,
it came to daylight on the
other side of the mountain.

73

And soon, the train came through the mountain and onto the great green plain beyond.

And on went the train,
on and on,
down its long steel track.

And the smoke trailed back,
and back,
and back.

75

One More Rabbit ...

Illustrated by
Emma Levey

Once upon a time, in a hollow tree stump, lived **one** excited rabbit with ...

one
loving mother and ...   **one**
loving father and ...

two
helpful sisters and ...

three

not-so-helpful brothers and ...

four

music-loving
uncles and .

five

busy aunts and ...

85

six
trouble-making
cousins and ...

seven

impatient second cousins and ...

89

eight

merry third cousins and ...

two
grooving grandmothers and ...

two

grooving grandfathers and ...

four talented great-grandmothers and ...

four talented great-grandfathers and ...

eight toe-tapping
great-great-grandmothers and ...

eight toe-tapping
great-great-grandfathers and ...

one
delicious
birthday
carrot cake.
It didn't
last long ...

99

They were a BIG, warm rabbit family,
all in one clump.

And they all celebrated together
in a hollow tree stump ...

with a little excited rabbit
who was learning how to jump!

The Fish with the Deep Sea Smile

Illustrated by

Henry Fisher

They fished
and they fished,

Way down in the sea.

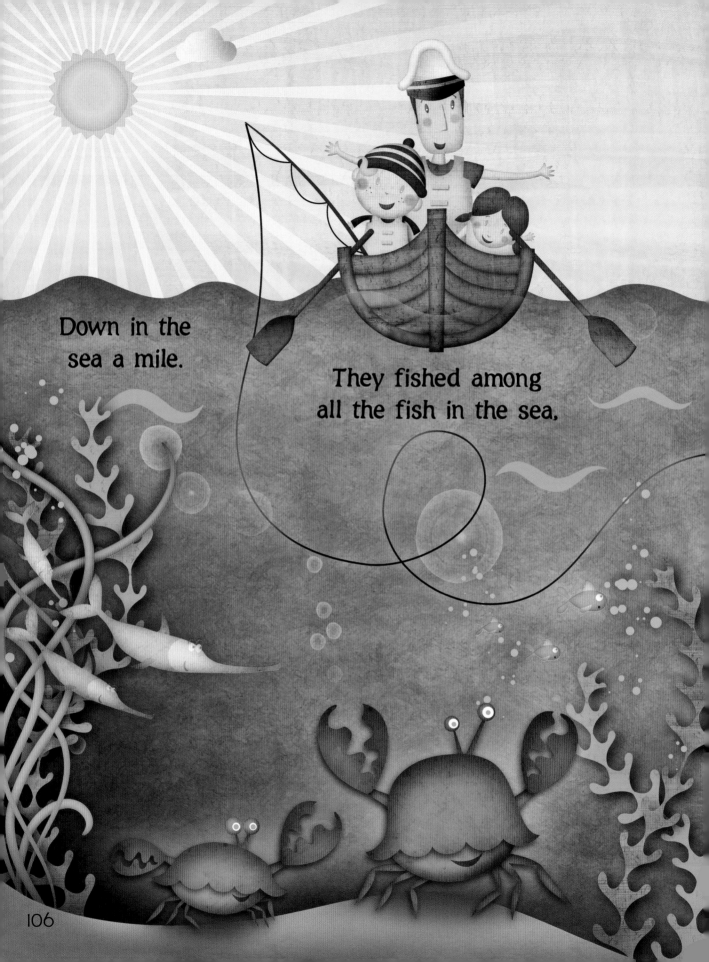

Down in the
sea a mile.

They fished among
all the fish in the sea.

For the fish with the
deep sea smile.

One fish came up
from the deep of the sea,

From down in the sea a mile.
It had blue-green eyes
and whiskers three,

But never a deep sea smile.

One fish came up
from the deep of the sea,
From down in the sea a mile,

With electric lights
up and down its tail,
But never a deep sea smile.

They fished
and they fished,
All across the sea,
And down in the depths a mile.
They fished among all the fish in the sea,

For the fish with
the deep sea smile.

One fish came up with
terrible teeth,

One fish with a long, strong jaw.

They fished all through the ocean deep,
For many and many a mile.

And they caught a fish
with a laughing eye,

But none
with a
deep sea
smile.

117

And then, one day,
they got a pull,

From down in the
sea a mile.

And when they pulled
the fish into the boat,

He smiled a
deep sea smile.

And as he smiled, the hook got free,
And then, what a **deep sea smile!**

He flipped his tail
and swam away,

Down in the sea a mile.

all the little Fathers

Illustrated by
Marilyn Faucher

All the bear fathers were catching fish with their children.

All the dog fathers were giving their
children bones to chew.

All the squirrel fathers were
hiding nuts for their children.

All the lion fathers were
roaring with their children.

133

All the monkey fathers

were hanging out with their children.

All the bird fathers were bringing
food to their hungry children.

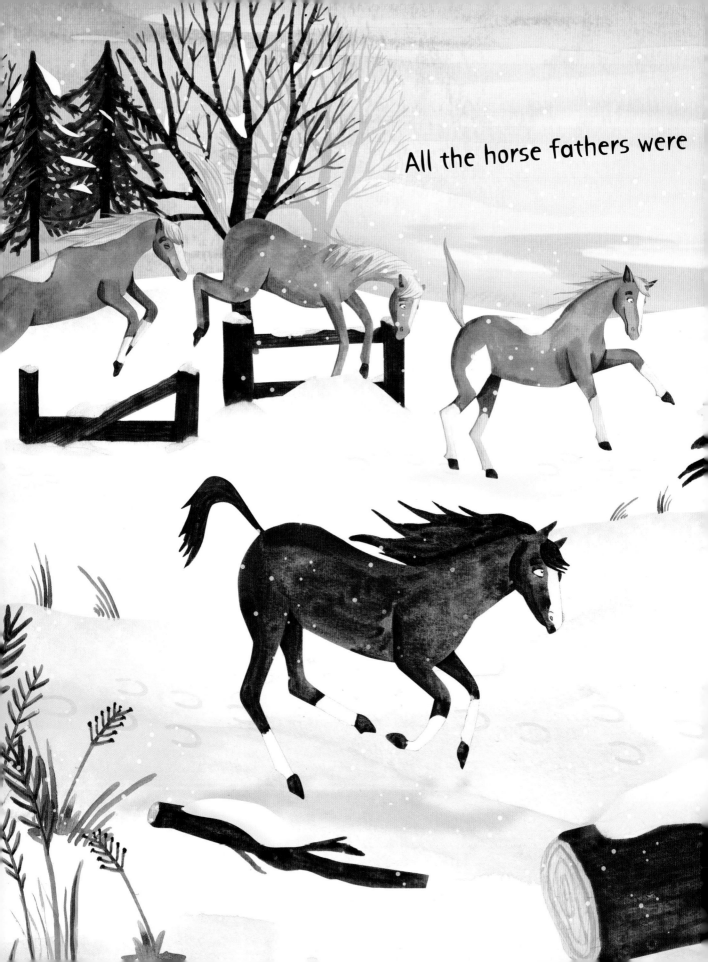

All the horse fathers were

leaping with their children.

All the cat fathers were purring to their children.

140

All the rabbit fathers were hopping

home with their children.

All the little fathers were
putting their children to bed.

144

Wish
upon a
dream

Illustrated by
Charlotte Cooke

Sleep, little squirrel,
and dream your dream,
Of nuts that fall and the
trickling stream.

Sleep, little rabbit, the carrot grows,
In the garden and under your nose.

Sleep, little horse, the day is over,
Dream of fields covered with clover.

The children dream of hammers and nails,
And spinning tops and boats with sails.

The little girl dreams of clouds up high,
And rabbits and horses that leap through the sky.

For everyone, the world is a wish,

For the child,

the rabbit,

and the fish.

Wish upon your dreams tonight,
And may your dreams last till daylight.

The fish must dream of more and more water,

Of a dolphin's niece
and a turtle's daughter.

159

The little bird dreams of endless song,
Sung in the branches all night long.

The little mouse dreams of another mouse,
Tucked up warm in a tiny house.

As you are falling deep into sleep,
In your heart, your hopes you keep.

So, wish upon your dreams tonight,
And may your dreams last till daylight.

Night comes along without a sound,
With soft, dark shadows all around.

Dreaming child, what you shall see

Deep in sleep might someday be.

The Good Little Bad Little Pig!

Illustrated by
Loretta Schauer

One day, a little boy named Peter asked his mother if he could have a pig.

"What!" said Peter's mother. "You want a dirty little, bad little pig?"

"No," said Peter. "I want a clean little pig. And I don't want a bad little pig or a good little pig. I want a good little, bad little pig."

"I've never heard of a clean little pig," said Peter's mother, "but let's try to find one."

So they sent a letter to a farmer who owned some pigs:

Farmer, Farmer
I want a pig
Not ~~to~~ too little
And not too big

Not too good
And not too bad
The ~~for~~ very best pig

No!

That the mother Pig had.

Peter

173

The farmer had five little pigs that lived in an old,
muddy pigpen with an old mother sow.

When the farmer read Peter's letter, he looked at his five little pigs.
Three good little pigs were fast asleep.

One bad little pig was
jumping up and down.

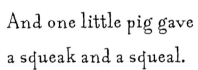

And one little pig gave
a squeak and a squeal.

"That," said the farmer, "is a good little, bad little pig." And he grabbed the little pig and sent him to Peter.

When Peter's mother saw the pig, she said,
"What a dirty little pig!"
The pig said,

"Squeeeeeeeeeeee-ump-ump-ump!"

But Peter said, "Wait till he's
had a bath."

But then the little pig jumped out of the box and ran around, squealing like a fire engine.

"What a bad little pig!" said Peter's father and his grandmother.

"He is not a bad little pig," said Peter.

"Wait until he gets to know us."

The little pig stared at Peter out of
his little eyes. Then he shook himself
and trotted after Peter.

"What a good little pig!" said Peter's grandmother, and she gave the little pig a bowl of bread and milk to eat.

"Wait," said Peter. "Remember, this is a good little, bad little pig."

"Galumph-gump gump gump gump."

The little pig made snuffling, sneezing noises as he ate.

"What terrible table manners!" said Peter's grandmother. "What a **bad** little pig!"

"Come on, you **good** little, bad little pig," said Peter. "I will give you a bath."

Peter put the little pig into a bathtub full of warm water and rubbed him with a big bar of white soap. "What a mess!" said Peter's mother. "What a bad little pig!"

Peter scrubbed and rubbed until the pure white
soapsuds were all black and the little pig was all clean,
from the tip of his tail to the tip of his nose.

Then, Peter took the little pig
for a walk.

"Look," said Peter to the policeman. "Did you ever see such a fine little, clean little pig?"

"No," said the policeman. "What a good little pig." He blew his whistle and stopped all the cars, so that Peter and the little pig could cross the road.

The little pig did not want to cross the road. Peter pulled on the leash, but the little pig refused to budge.

"What a bad little pig!"

The people in their cars
began to honk their horns.

So the policeman pushed, and Peter pulled the pig into the road.

"Squeak-squeeeeeeee-ump -ump-ump!"

Then, suddenly, the little pig trotted on, as nice as you please.
"What a good little pig," said the people in the cars as they
went on their way.

And so it was that Peter got just what he wanted:
a **good** little, **bad** little pig.

Sometimes the little pig was **good**,
and sometimes he was **bad**,

but he was **the best** little pig
a little boy could **ever have.**

EVER!

Oink!